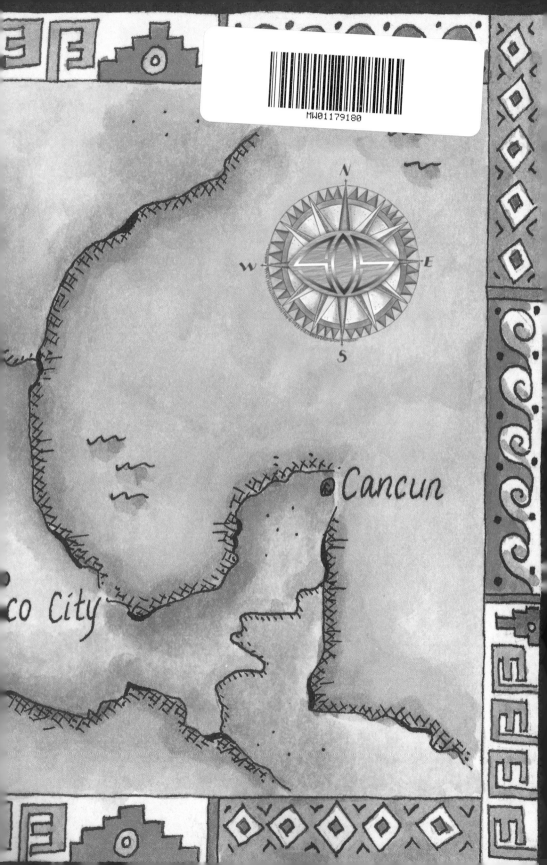

Cancun

co City

For more information about the Save Our Seas Foundation,
please visit our website at
www.SaveOurSeas.com

Book designed and packaged by Jokar Productions

For information regarding permission, write to Save Our Seas Foundation,
Attention: Permissions Department, 6 rue Bellot, 1206 Geneva, Switzerland

ISBN 978-0-9800444-1-6

©2008 Jokar Productions, LLC
Photography/Tom Campbell

10 9 8 7 6 5 4 3 2 1

Printed China

THE DEVIL FISH

by Geoffrey T. Williams

Photography/Tom Campbell

Illustrated by
Artful Doodlers

save our seas
FOUNDATION

THE DEVIL FISH

ONE

MEETING WITH A GIANT

Tyler was a little nervous.

You might be too with a fifteen-meter shark swimming toward you with its nearly one-and-a-half-meter mouth wide open.

What would you do? Swim to get out of its way? Wave frantically to try and scare it off? Signal your dive buddy to come to your rescue?

Tyler, of course, did none of these things. He was right where he wanted to be – off Corralvo Island in the Sea of Cortez, Baja, California, staring adventure in the face.

He keyed the wireless microphone built into his full face mask. "You see the size of this guy?"

His twin sister Alena was floating on the surface nearby. "Actually, I think this *guy* is a girl. I hope you're getting her on tape."

The power-sled with the hi-definition video camera hovered in front of the boy, capturing every move of the biggest fish either of them had ever seen.

"Gotta be close to fifteen meters long," he said. "Good thing I'm not on her menu."

The shark's wide, flat head swiveled back and forth. As it opened and closed its huge mouth, it sucked in liters of seawater along with the countless tiny zooplankton that *were* on its menu. Zooplankton are microscopic animals that are a primary food source for some of the ocean's biggest animals such as humpback whales and whale sharks.

"You do a *Jonah* and get swallowed," his sister said, "I'm not coming after you."

No chance, Tyler thought. Whale sharks are gentle giants – big, slow-moving, even sometimes curious around divers, and not dangerous. *But she sure is big. And beautiful.* Slate blue with a dim, crosshatch pattern of stripes, lines and spots on top, with a pale white belly. *The Foundation's going to love this.*

The *Foundation* is the Save Our Seas Foundation in Switzerland. Tyler and Alena Worthy are two of the three members of the Foundation's A.I. team (in case you don't know, A.I. stands for Aquatic Intervention). They're troubleshooters for the Foundation in the oceans around the world. Pollution, illegal fishing, dying coral reefs, you name it, the A.I. team is ready to go anywhere and do anything to help.

Brutus, the third member of the team, was currently whining and wearing a path, back and forth, on the deck of the *Sea Worthy*, their big hydrofoil, floating a few meters above all the fun.

As usual, Brutus was upset at being left behind. The twins had patiently explained to him that, while whale sharks didn't normally eat small Jack Russel terriers, he could get sucked in along with the zooplankton – you know, kind of by accident – and the giant probably wouldn't even notice.

The sky was blue, the air was warm. The water was clear and calm. There were his teammates, right over there, having all the fun. And here he was, stuck on the boat. Again.

Maybe Brutus didn't believe the twins. Maybe he'd already forgotten their warning.

Or, maybe he just didn't care.

With a small bark he launched himself into the water.

Right into the path of the whale shark.

The next moments were very busy.

Brutus, happily dog-paddling toward Tyler, had no idea the whale shark, its mouth gaping wide, was closing in behind him.

Tyler, busy video taping, didn't notice the dog.

Alena and the shark spotted the dog at the same time.

Alena screamed, "Brutus!"

Of course, she was screaming into her mask, so all that came out was a cloud of bubbles and something that sounded like "B-b-b-r-r-r-d-z!"

Almost lazily, the shark dove under the small dog, missing him easily.

Alena swam over and put her arm around Brutus – who had no idea how close he'd come to getting to know the whale shark from the inside – and began swimming back to the ship.

Tyler got the whole thing in beautiful, high-definition video. It would eventually make it onto their "Best of the Worthy's" highlight tape, and send the whole family into fits of laughter every time they watched it.

Of course, Brutus never found anything funny about it at all.

Who would have guessed a week ago, the team would be here, diving in the Sea of Cortez, instead of home in Santa Barbara, studying for tests?

Two

Xochitl and the Voice of Adventure

*O*ne week earlier…

The sun was glancing off the small waves in Santa Barbara harbor. The air was warm. The *Sea Worthy* was rocking gently. School was ending. Summer was on the way. Time for adventure, excitement, discovery, not homework.

But it seemed even adventure has to wait for a math final.

The lounge aboard the ship was comfortable and quiet. A relaxing place to study.

Maybe too relaxing.

Tyler yawned, then read, "An object is launched at 19.6 meters per second from a 58.8-meter tall platform. The equation for the object's height *s* at time *t* seconds after launch is $s(t) = -4.9t2 + 19.6t + 58.8$, where *s* is in meters. When does the object strike the ground?"

Alena yawned along with her brother. "Right after my head hits my desk." Her eyes were closing and her head was nodding. They'd been at it for hours. "Give me a few minutes – "

Just then, the voice of adventure burst into the lounge.

"*This is an AI Notice. You have incoming live-video. Repeat. You have incoming live-video.*" It was the computer voice of the Foundation's alert system.

"Just in time." Slamming the math book shut, Tyler jumped up and switched on the large, high-definition monitor. A girl's face appeared. "It's Show!" he said.

Her name was Xochitl Meléndez. Her unusual first name was pronounced *Shosh-EET-L* in the Nahuatl language spoken by the ancient Aztecs. All her friends called her *Show*. The twins were two of her best friends.

She was the Foundation's contact in Baja California.

"Am I interrupting anything important?" she said.

"No! No. Of course not," the twins said at the same time.

"Do you have an emergency for us?" Tyler said.

"Yeah," said Alena. "Something that means we have to drop everything and head down to help you?"

Show grinned. She could see the table behind the twins littered with books and papers. "Studying for finals?"

"Well – "

"I can call back in a couple of weeks – "

"No. No. No. That's okay," Tyler said. "What's up?"

"It's not an emergency, and it may be nothing. I don't have any hard evidence, but a fisherman out of Bahia La Paz reported seeing a couple of mantas off Isla Cerralvo a few days ago."

That was big news. For years, schools of giant mantas could be found around the island almost all the time. Then, about five years ago, they all disappeared. No one knew where they had gone. Or why.

"The Foundation wants us to check it out."

The twins looked at each other, thinking identical thoughts.

"We can take our tests online—" Tyler said.

"Like we did when we were in South Africa—" Alena said.

"You're sure?"

"Oh, yeah," said Tyler.

"Positive," said Alena.

THREE

A.I. ON THE WAY

The Worthy's were finishing a family conference in the living room. A huge window stretched across the room with a sweeping view down the mountainside to the city, scattered like toy building blocks far below. The *Sea Worthy* was a speck of white against the blue of the harbor.

Sheryl Worthy smiled. "Of course you have to go," she said. "This is important." She turned to her husband, "Remember – "

"The first time we took them down to dive with the mantas?" their father, Peter Worthy, said. "I'll never forget." He looked at the twins. "I think that's when you fell in love with the sea. If you can help the mantas you have to go."

"And tell Show it's been too long since her last visit," Mrs. Worthy said.

Mr. Worthy grinned, "And way too long since we had her enchiladas molé."

A short time later the twins had worked out a schedule with their teachers and arranged to meet Show in Bahia La Paz.

Hydraulic motors whined, servos clicked and hummed, and the *Sea Worthy* was transformed from a sleek, fast, boat into a sleek, much faster jet plane.

Tyler was running through the takeoff checklist.

Alena was below, securing their equipment. *Arky* was firmly fixed to a bulkhead in one corner. Their personal submarine, the *Nous Venons*, was locked down in the hold. The super-computer and all the lab equipment was safely stowed.

She hurried up to the lounge to check their food and other supplies, double-checking that there were a couple of boxes of *Walker's Stem Ginger Biscuits* aboard. They all loved the snack cookies, fighting over the smallest crumbs.

Tyler's voice came over the intercom. "Make sure all seatbacks are in an upright position and all luggage is stowed in the overhead bins. Crew members prepare for takeoff – "

Very funny, Alena thought.

" – and please note the position of the air sickness bags in case of – well, air sickness."

She sighed. *It's going to be a long trip.*

Tyler was ready for takeoff when she got up to the bridge. Brutus was in his custom-built chair, seatbelt fastened, wearing a small helmet and earphones, and looking every bit the team's honorary communication's officer.

Alena buckled up and Tyler pushed the throttles forward. The powerful engines roared.

Moments later they were in the air, speeding south on another SOS adventure.

FOUR

RETURN OF THE DEVIL FISH

The day after their encounter with the whale shark, the twins picked up Show in Bahia La Paz and headed out into the Gulf of Baja, hoping to spot giant mantas.

The water around Isla Cerralvo was a wonderland of sea life.

In addition to the giant whale shark, the team catalogued white tipped reef sharks, a school of hammerhead sharks, moray eels, pufferfish, angelfish, barberfish, stonefish, swordfish, sailfish, groupers, and many, many others.

A pod of humpback whales passed within meters of the *Sea Worthy* one day and Tyler was lucky enough to get some video of one of the huge animals breaching—the sight of a 20-meter-long, 30-ton whale leaping out of the water was always a thrill.

A pair of playful dolphins nearly always accompanied the team when they were in the water. They became so familiar that Alena gave them names: *Chipper* and *Chirp*, because of the sounds they made. They stuck their snouts out of the water and held long conversations with Brutus, chipping and chirping at the dog, while he yipped and yapped from the deck of the *Sea Worthy*. Just like they were friends.

During their dives the team saw plenty of small rays, including bullseye electric rays, Cortez round stingrays, diamond stingrays. But, after a week, there was no sign of giant mantas.

Show couldn't hide her disappointment. "It would mean so much to have the mantas come back. People used to come here just to see them and swim with them. It was good for the economy. And Mexican law protects them now, so there's no more hunting."

"Let's give it another day," Alena said. "Then we'll have to head back."

The next morning the three of them tumbled off the dive platform into the water off the northern end of the island, and floated down through the blue. Tyler was carrying the tagging equipment he brought along on every dive. He planned on using it to attach a small GPS transmitter to a manta so they could follow its movements and learn more about the beautiful, mysterious animals. Mantas are close relatives of sharks, but their pectoral fins had evolved into large wings, and on opposite sides of their wide mouths are lobes, used to scoop up the plankton they feed on. These lobes look a little like horns, and that's why some people call them Devil Fish.

If you're ever lucky enough to see a manta, you'll know immediately: they're diamond-shaped, and the adults are huge, weighing as much as 3000 kilos, their wings sometimes spreading more than 6 meters across. It's magical to watch them. They circle, spiral, and glide through the water like ballet dancers, their wide mouths open to take in plankton. They also seem to enjoy the company of divers, occasionally swimming right up next to them.

The team was drifting on a warm, slow current only 5 or 10 meters below the surface. The bright Baja sun knifed through the water, throwing shimmering streamers of light and shadow onto the reef below.

Shadows blocked the sunlight.

Show looked up. Directly overhead were two huge diamond-shapes, gliding slowly past, just below the surface, like black and white angels.

She keyed her microphone. "Don't look now, but we have company."

The twins looked up.

"Wow," Alena said. "Tyler, did you bring a camera? If we get a picture of their markings, we can identify them later." Every manta has unique markings which can be used to identify individuals.

"No camera, but I bet I can get close enough to tag one."

"A male and a female," Show said. "And it looks like the female might be pregnant." She was trying to memorize the patches of dark markings on the mantas' pale bellies. The male had a stripe of black crossing its belly, while the female had several rounded teardrop shapes on hers.

Tyler slowly swam up behind the male, who didn't seem the least bit nervous. Carefully, the boy extended the rod with the GPS transmitter toward the thickest part of one of the manta's wings. The transmitter had a small hook on it that allowed it to be harmlessly attached to the animal. After a period of time, the hook would deteriorate and the device would fall off, hopefully after broadcasting information to the Foundation's satellites about the animal's migration patterns, diving depths, water temperatures, and other important information.

With a quick thrust, Tyler attached the transmitter to the thickest part of the manta's wing, startling the animal, but not hurting him at all. With a dip of his powerful wings, the creature moved away, followed by the female, until they were both swallowed up in the shadows sliding across the reef.

FIVE

MUSTACHE PETE

After spotting the mantas, the excitement in the lounge that evening added extra spice to dinner.

Whenever they were with Show the twins begged her to cook authentic Mexican food. Tonight it was Café Xochitl Pollo Molé Poblano.

"Mustache Pete," Show said.

"What?" Alena said.

"The male. The black stripe looked kind of like a mustache."

"Oh, sure. Okay then, we should call the female 'Teardrop' because of her markings."

"I wonder why all the mantas disappeared," Show said. "And why these have come back."

"Maybe the dead zone drove them away," Tyler said, taking a huge bite of his chicken and cheese enchilada, dripping in spicy chocolate molé sauce.

Alena looked at him. "That old TV show? Gee, I kind of liked it."

Tyler boggled at his sister and forgot he had a mouthful of runny cheese and sauce. "Not *that* dead zone."

Alena watched a brown blob of molé sauce trickle down his chin. "That is so gross."

Show laughed. "You know he means the ocean dead zones, Alena.

All the farming over in the Yaqui River Valley has been causing fertilizer run-off into the Sea of Cortez, and massive growths of algae in the water. All that algae uses up huge amounts of oxygen, and there's not enough left over for the coral and the fish, so they die."

"And," said Tyler, wiping his chin, "The algae causes red and brown tides that poison oyster and other shellfish beds."

"Scientists think that's what killed all those sea lions in Northern California a few years ago. Anyway," Show said. "Some of the algae growths from Yaqui drifted over to this side of the gulf."

"Maybe we could take the *Nous Venons* out to get some samples and – "

Whatever plans they were about to make were interrupted. Brutus, who had been patiently waiting for something good to fall off the table, bounced up and barked as a shrill alarm went off.

"*This is an AI Red Alert. This is not a drill. Repeat. This is an AI Red Alert.*"

Six

Ghost Net

The big monitor glowed to life and the face of Dr. Andreas Potterat, the Foundation's Chief Research Scientist came on the screen. He looked even more serious than usual.

"We've got a fix on your manta. I'm uploading the tracking data now."

Show clapped her hands in excitement. "That's great news."

"Maybe. But the satellites picked up something else. I was analyzing an image we picked up off Isla Socorro in the Islas Revillagigedo (Ree-vee-ah-hee-HAY-do) archipelago, maybe 500 kilometers from where you are now. We couldn't see a lot of detail, and couldn't find it again on the next pass, but we need you to check it out."

"What?" said Show.

"We're afraid it's a drift net. A ghost drift net."

Alena shuddered at the words. Driftnets have been called "walls of death, " and of all the destructive fishing methods ever invented, this is the worst.

Here's how it works: a fishing boat in the high seas drops a net into the water. A net that might be more than 65 kilometers long and 12 meters high. It has floats along the top, and weights along the bottom to hold it vertical. The boat then leaves the net to drift with the current,

trapping anything that swims into it – whether it's legal fish such as tuna and wahoo, or protected animals. So over the years millions of cetaceans – dolphins, porpoises, and whales – along with seals, sharks, sea birds, and sea turtles, have met horrible deaths, caught, trapped, and drowned in these nearly invisible, deadly, nylon spider webs.

The United Nations passed a resolution banning their use and now drift nets are against the law in almost every country in the world, including Mexico, but there are problems. The laws are hard to enforce on the high seas; many of the boats disguise their illegal fishing methods; and worst or all, some boats just abandon the nets, leaving them in the ocean, untended, and unaccounted for, drifting, catching, and killing indiscriminately.

These are the *ghost nets.*

Eventually the nets become so filled with dead animals, they sink to the bottom, carrying the bodies of the unfortunate victims with them.

Dr. Potterat said, "What makes this even worse – "

"It gets worse?" said Tyler."

"Your manta seems to be heading in the same direction."

The waters of the archipelago are home to a wide variety of sea creatures. Ancient undersea volcanoes pushed the islands up from the ocean bed, warming the surrounding waters, and providing a rich environ-ment for mantas, schools of hammerhead, silky, whitetip, and Galapagos sharks, even whale sharks, along with countless beautiful reef fish, eels, and octopus.

If the net was drifting through the islands of the archipelago, a tragedy was in the making.

"Nous venons," Tyler said softy.

We're coming.

SEVEN

TRAVELLING COMPANIONS

They set off at sunrise the next morning.

While Tyler piloted, Alena worked in the lounge, scanning radio frequencies, trying to pick up signals from the transmitter attached to the manta. Sometime during the night, the signal had disappeared. Chances are, the manta was too deep for the transmitter to work. But she couldn't be sure. So far, nothing.

Show was monitoring data from the Foundation's satellites, trying to get a current position for the ghost net. She wasn't having any better luck.

The blistered moonscape of the Baja peninsula streamed by on their starboard side. The girls were too busy to see much of it. But Tyler, at the wheel, loved it. He found it strangely beautiful – much of it barren desert with a few straggling bushes and thin trees. He saw a cluster of giant Cardon cactus, several more than 20 meters tall. The sunburned hills and rocky cliffs that plunged abruptly into the water were in stark contrast to the crystal blue waters of the Sea of Cortez.

They were coming up to Land's End at the tip of the peninsula, and Cabo San Lucas with its sea-sculpted rock formations: El Arco (the arch) and El Dedo de Dios (the finger of God). Now and then, patches of bright green appeared against the brown landscape. Resorts and golf courses. Cabo was a popular place for deep water fishermen and sun-starved tourists from the north.

Brutus's barking caused Tyler to glance over the side. He smiled and called down to Alena, "We've got company. Take a look off port."

She walked over to the left side of the lounge in time to see Chipper and Chirp gracefully arcing through the air and plunging into the water alongside the *Sea Worthy*.

Maybe the dog and the dolphins really *were* friends.

The playful animals stayed with the boat all the way past Cabo. When the *Sea Worthy* rounded the point, they leaped and chirped, then swam off to swim and play somewhere else.

Brutus's tail sank between his little hind legs. He obviously missed them.

Late the next afternoon Isla Socorrro appeared on the western horizon.

Still no signal from the manta.

And, more ominous, no sign of the ghost net.

EIGHT

NEEDLES AND HAYSTACKS

The *Sea Worthy* was anchored near Cabo Regla, off the southern tip of Isla Socorro, one of the four small islands in the archipelago—an archipelago is a group, or chain of islands—which included Isla San Benedicto, Isla Roca Partida, Isla Clarion, and Isla Socorro. Show had alerted the Mexican Naval base on the island about the drift net, and they had promised to aid in the search.

Socorro is the Spanish word for *help.* And, right now, the team needed all the *socorro* it could get.

Tyler's eyes were bloodshot from looking at dozens of satellite photos of the ocean surrounding the four islands. "It's just ocean. It all looks the same. I think we're looking for a needle in a haystack."

Show nodded, a little depressed. The thought of mantas and other sea creatures being caught in the net was very troubling. "We might never find it."

Alena was not willing to give up, and was scanning more images. "The Foundation's trained all its satellites on the area. Every time they fly over they take more pictures. We just have to keep on looking—"

"—for a needle in a haystack," Tyler said.

"Well, it *is* a 30-kilometer long needle," said Show.

"In a 150-thousand square kilometer haystack," said Tyler.

Alena was thinking. "We could send Arky to look, but it would take him days to cover the area. We need to narrow the search somehow."

Show's face brightened. She had an idea. She moved to the large monitor. "Turn on the Smartboard software."

Tyler pushed a button and the large screen turned into a hi-resolution computer monitor showing Show's computer desktop. She launched a search engine and in a few moments the team was looking at a detailed photograph of a drift net from the Foundation's image bank.

The Smartboard allowed her to draw on the screen with special pens. She circled parts of the net. "These floats that keep the net vertical in the water are shaped kind of like footballs. Very distinctive. And they're what – maybe two meters apart—?"

Tyler knew where she was going with this. "In a 30-kilometer long net there would be thousands of them—"

Alena had figured it out too. "—all strung out together in a line, floating on the surface. It wouldn't look like anything natural at all. It would be an anomaly."

Tyler felt hope for the first time in hours. "I think you're onto something, Show."

"Let's take another look at those satellite photos," the girl said.

"Look at this," Alena said. She had lined up three satellite photos on the screen. "These were taken on flybys over Roca Partida."

Tyler and Show moved closer. "Split Rock Island," Show said, using the English translation for Isla Roca Partida, the smallest of the four islands – actually just a couple of tall rocks jutting out of the ocean from the submerged peak of an old volcano.

Alena said. "Taken six hours apart as the satellite passed overhead."

Alena pointed at something in the first photo.

"There," she said. Her finger traced a thin, slightly fuzzy line that

curved like a snake. Then she pointed to something similar in the next picture. "And there, taken on the next pass. And the last one, taken about an hour ago." In each photo, the line was a little closer to the island.

"Might be our ghost net," said Show.

Tyler pointed to something near one of the rocks. "Yeah, but what's that?"

Show said, "Could be a tourist dive boat."

Alena, the team's digital image expert, said, "Let me zoom in and enhance the picture." She used some special software tools and the image got bigger and more distinct.

Show gasped. "*That's* no tourist boat."

"Not with those big hoists on deck," Tyler said. "You don't suppose—"

"Maybe now we know where that ghost net came from," Show said.

"Maybe it's not a *ghost* net after all," Alena said. "Maybe that boat is fishing illegally. The archipelago is now a protected Marine Biosphere, and no fishing is allowed around the islands. We need to send Arky and get some close-ups."

Show nodded her head. "And we need to alert the naval base."

NINE

ARKY II

The lights of the lab gleamed on the tall, shiny tube strapped to the bulkhead.

Inside was a mirror-bright titanium cylinder. It could be mistaken for a missile, except for the thick, rounded dome of plexiglass on top which covered a camera lens. There was an inset control panel with lights, buttons, and an LED screen that was now dark.

Tyler touched the screen. After a moment it lit up with the words "HELLO" in bright green letters. As Tyler watched, the camera lens came to life. It swiveled, and focused on the boy. "Hello, Tyler Worthy," said a computer-generated voice.

"Hello, Arky. How are you?"

"All systems. Are go."

"We have a mission for you."

"Mission. Good." Arky was a nickname. Much easier to remember, and say, than *Autonomous Aerial Reconnaissance Craft*. Actually, this was Arky the Second. Arky the First had been destroyed crashing into a pirate's boat in South Africa. It just so happened that when he crashed, he sank the boat and helped save the A.I. team's lives.

A hatch in the ceiling opened and the hydraulic lift raised Arky to the deck. Within minutes he was speeding toward tiny Roca Partida, more than 100 kilometers away.

TEN

RACE

I found him!" Alena said.

"Mustache Pete?" Show moved to the communication console to look over her shoulder.

"Look." Alena pointed to a blinking point of light on one of the screens. Readouts for latitude and longitude were displayed next to it.

"You think both of the mantas are there?"

"Probably. You know how mantas love it around these islands."

Suddenly, Show had a bad feeling. "What's the lat and long for Roca Partida?"

Alena checked. "Oh, no. The locations are almost overlapping. The manta and the drift net look like they're moving toward each other."

She quickly showed Tyler the problem.

"Can we fly?" asked Show.

Tyler shook his head. "Not enough fuel. We'll have to motor."

Within minutes the powerful engines of the *Sea Worthy* rumbled to life, and the team was speeding toward the distant island.

"We're not going to make it," Show said, looking over at Alena.

The girls were standing near the bow, straining to see ahead, their hair streaming back from the speed of the *Sea Worthy*. But Isla Roca Partida was still over 75 kilometers away and invisible below the horizon.

"We have to make it," Alena said. "I'm going below to see if Arky's sending any pictures back yet." The *Sea Worthy* was making top speed, almost 50 kilometers an hour, while Arky was capable of sustained speeds of over 400. The tiny aircraft would be over the island long before the A.I. team got there.

At the comm console Alena flipped a few switches and turned on a microphone.

"Arky?"

"Hello, Alena Worthy," said the small computer voice.

"We're looking for a commercial fishing boat."

The Foundation's database included thousands of images of ships and boats which Arky could rummage through in a microsecond. In another microsecond he could identify the type, manufacturer, size, cargo hold capacity, and usually, the country of origin. So far, Arky's camera was showing nothing but the vast, empty ocean streaming by in a blur.

After a tense minute or two, the jagged rocks of Isla Roca Partida poked above the horizon.

Moment by moment the rocks grew larger on the screen.

Show sat down next to Alena and intently watched the blinking dot that was the manta transmitter. They wouldn't receive another update on the possible location of the drift net until the next satellite fly-by, still several hours away. It was nerve-wracking not knowing exactly where the deadly net was.

Brutus barked once and gazed at the images the aircraft was sending back.

"Alena Worthy," Arky said.

"What is it, Arky?" There was still no sign of a boat on the screen.

"Anomaly. Alena Worthy. Anomaly." An anomaly meant Arky had found something unusual, something out of place.

"Slow down, Arky. You're going too fast for me to see."

"Slow down. Good." The blurred whitecaps came into focus and became individual waves.

"Display, Arky."

"Display. Good." Arky dropped until he was flying less than fifty meters above the water. He tilted and turned in a wide, slow circle, until the anomaly came into view.

"Zoom in."

"Zoom. Good." Arky zoomed his camera in for a close-up view.

Show was intent on the image. "There! That's it! There it is!"

Arky had located the long trail of floats that marked the drift net.

"Location, Arky," Alena said.

Arky stored the latitude and longitude in his memory and, at the same time, sent the coordinates to the *Sea Worthy*.

Show gasped. "The manta's almost on top of the net!"

They were still more than an hour away.

ELEVEN

LOST AND FOUND

I've lost him," Show said. "I've lost the signal." She had been monitoring the manta, checking its location. But the transmission had died.

"The GPS unit might have fallen off," Tyler said. "Or the battery failed. But you have the last known position, right?"

Meanwhile, Arky was speeding toward Isla Roca Partida. The tall rocks rushed to fill the screen.

Arky circled, his lens swiveling back and forth, searching for the fishing boat – "Alert. Alena Worthy. Alert," Arky had located the ship.

"I see it Arky. Good work." Of course Arky was just a machine, and immune to compliments, but he was so smart it was easy for the team to think of him as something more.

Show radioed the naval base on Isla Socorro, "Aquí está la localización del barco de pesca." She repeated the boat's location.

"Estamos viniendo," the officer said. *We're coming.*

Then she went back to searching for the lost manta signal.

The fishing boat was fifty meters of rust and peeling paint. Its dirty decks were littered with scraps of net, broken floats, and unidentifiable junk. Several large hoists — used to lower and raise the huge drift nets — were visible at the stern .

As Arky circled, two men came out of the wheelhouse, pointing at the small plane and shouting at each other. They had never seen anything quite like Arky and didn't know what to make of the drone. After a minute or two they seemed to conclude that whatever Arky was, he wasn't good news for them.

The rusty boat trembled as the engines started. With as much speed as it could make, it fled Isla Roca Partida, abandoning the deadly drift net.

Twelve

Drifting Death

Tyler watched on the monitor as the *Nous Venons* slipped out of the hold and onto the surface of the ocean. He switched on the microphone. "You're clear."

Alena answered, "We're going to follow the line of the net. See how long it is, and see if we can find the manta."

"Don't you get tangled up."

"The *Nous Venons* is plenty strong enough to pull us out of trouble."

The small sub picked up speed as it left the mother ship.

A short time later they came to a section of the net where the floats had been pulled under the water. Alena brought the sub to a stop and lowered a high-resolution camera to scan underneath them. The images on the monitor were something out of a nightmare. Both girls were quiet. Neither had ever seen such deliberate and pointless destruction.

Turtles, several porpoises, a large tiger shark, along with wahoo and tuna, were trapped and dying, or already dead, in the net. It was the weight of so many dead animals that had pulled the floats under.

Finally, Show said, "Some of them may still be alive. We have to do something."

Alena tied the sub up to one of the nearby floats still on the surface.

Minutes later she finished pulling on her fins while Show shrugged into her scuba harness and adjusted her mask.

Brutus barked.

"Sorry, boy. Someone has to stay aboard while we check out the net. There might be animals trapped in it that are still alive."

The small dog whined, but seemed to understand. He watched as the girls rocked backward off the sub and into the water.

Thirteen

The Trail of Teardrops

A pinging sound rang through the lounge and Tyler rushed over to the comm console. A signal from the manta's transmitter, and there on the screen the blinking dot with the location.

Directly beneath the *Sea Worthy*!

Tyler picked up the microphone to alert Alena and Show but received no answer. *Maybe they're in the water. That's where I need to be.*

He rushed out of the lounge and frantically began sorting through the equipment locker. He pulled on a scuba tank, weight belt, flippers, and mask.

Then, for the first time in his life, he broke the most important rule of underwater diving: *never dive alone.*

He tumbled off the dive platform and the water closed over his head.

The water was clear and warm near the surface. He could see almost 50 meters. At any other time he would have taken pleasure in how beautiful it was around the small island – colorful fish, a school of wahoo near a ledge that dropped off to deeper water – but he didn't have time.

As he dropped lower, he became aware of how chilly he was getting, and realized he hadn't taken time to put on his wetsuit. Oh, well. He shouldn't be down here too long.

He knew the net was close, but couldn't see it. Just as the unfortunate animals who became trapped couldn't see it. He wondered what it would feel like – caught and helpless. Were they confused? Frightened? He knew he would be. He turned in a circle, bubbles from his tank rising overhead. The shadow of the *Sea Worthy* was no more than four or five meters above.

Another shadow passed overhead. A large, graceful, diamond-shape. A beautiful manta. He noticed two teardrop marking on the underside. Could this be the same manta they'd seen in the Sea of Cortez? Could she have made it so far in such a short amount of time? Had the two mantas traveled together? Where was she going? Tyler knew Moustache Pete and the drift net must be close. Should he follow Teardrop?

He kicked and followed the manta deeper.

The light dimmed. The water became colder. Suddenly the manta swerved, as though avoiding something. Slowly, a pale curtain of almost invisible nylon strands emerged from the shadows. Tyler had found the ghost net.

Fourteen

Collision Course

It was strangely quiet. The sea was flat and calm. There was almost no breeze. The *Sea Worthy* was quietly rocking on the water.

Brutus's claws clicked nervously on the deck as he paced back and forth, watching the spot where the girls had disappeared.

A high-pitched chirping sound broke the silence.

Brutus spun around. Two dolphins were hovering in the water right next to the *Nous Venons*. Brutus jumped and barked in excitement. Chipper and Chirp had found them.

Then, another sound caught the dog's attention. A distant, low, churning sound. He looked up from the dolphins to see a giant, rusted hulk of a ship heading right for the *Sea Worthy*.

Brutus had been trained long ago to warn the twins if something seemed wrong. He bounced up onto the sub's comm console and pushed the microphone button with his paw.

Fifteen meters below, Alena's earphones crackled to life. But the sound was confusing. Brutus was barking madly, and there seemed to be some kind of squealing whistle in the background. *What's going on?* She wondered.

She headed back up with Show right behind her.

As soon as they cleared the surface they were surprised by two dolphins swimming in a wide circle around them and chirping loudly. What were they so excited about?

Behind her, Show had ripped off her mask. She screamed, "Alena!"

Alena and saw the knife-edge bow of a ship, less than a hundred meters away, on a collision course with the *Sea Worthy*.

Fifteen

Life or Death

Tyler was looking at a graveyard of sea creatures, trapped and drowned by the ghost net. A huge hammerhead shark, at least 5 meters long, was a few meters away, and next to it, a giant manta. At first, Tyler thought the manta was dead, but then he saw it shudder and flex its wings.

Mustache Pete was alive, but barely. The beautiful creature was hopelessly snarled in the deadly strands of nylon.

Tyler shivered from the cold as he approached the manta. In addition to forgetting his wetsuit, he wasn't wearing a dive watch, so he had no idea how much time he had before he ran out of air.

When he got close enough he could see that the nylon netting had cut the manta's skin, and was deeply embedded in several places along its wings. This wasn't going to be easy.

Tyler pulled his dive knife and moved closer. The manta's mouth was opening and closing. Tyler watched as the large eyes swiveled toward him. It was impossible to tell what the manta was thinking or feeling, but the creature stopped struggling and seemed to be waiting.

SIXTEEN

IN HARM'S WAY

The prow of the approaching ship was like an axe blade falling toward them.

Alena knew they only had seconds before the collision. It was the fishing boat, of course. Whoever was at the wheel either didn't see the boat, or didn't care. Either way, it was about to slice the boat in half.

The noise from the approaching ship was deafening. The bow wave rolled and rocked the smaller vessel.

Show screamed and waved her arms at the dolphins. "Peligro! Peligro!" *Danger.*

Alena jammed the handles of the boat's engines all the way forward.

The boat surged ahead. It was going to be close.

The ship missed them by less than five meters. The bow wave rocked the *Sea Worthy*, sending a wall of water across its hull. Show grabbed a guard rail to keep from being washed overboard.

Brutus wasn't so lucky. The wave picked him up and tossed him into the ocean like a small stick.

SEVENTEEN

MAGIC CARPET RIDE

In. Hold. Out. Hold.

Tyler knew his air supply was running out. He was breathing shallowly while he cut the nylon netting. He was experienced enough to know he was in some trouble. Or would be soon. The worst part was no one knew where he was.

But he was so close to freeing the manta.

Finally the last strand parted. With a shrug, the manta drifted out of the trap. Tyler watched it slowly flex its wings. The cuts must hurt, but would certainly heal. Tyler had seen mantas off the coast of Mozambique with large shark bites on their wings swimming along normally.

In. Hold. Out. Hold.

As he started for the surface, his tank gave out the last breath of air.

He kicked harder, holding onto that last, precious bit of air. He knew it was dangerous to surface too fast, but what choice did he have? He knew he could hold his breath for almost two minutes.

He knew he could make it.

Looking up, he saw the surface was farther away than he had thought. In fact, it was dark up there. Wasn't it bright sunlight when he had started?

His vision was darkening. His chest began to ache. He knew in a matter of seconds his lungs would spasm and he would breathe in water. He kicked tiredly, but the surface seemed as far away as before. A roaring sound filled his ears. He closed his eyes against it.

That's when the dream started.

Alena fought to control the *Sea Worthy* as it tipped and tilted in the wash from the ship.

When the ship finally stabilized she saw Show gripping a guard rail and shouting. "Brutus! Pequeño perro. ¿Dónde estás? Brutus!" She looked back in panic at Alena. "He washed overboard. I can't see him."

Alena scanned the still roiling waters around them. Brutus was so small and the waves were so much bigger. How were they going to find him? Her eyes filled with tears. *No! He can't be gone! He saved our lives. He can't be gone!*

Both the girls heard the barking at the same time and turned to stare at an incredible sight.

Chipper and Chirp were arcing through the waves toward the boat. And balancing on the sleek grey back of one of the dolphins was Brutus.

The dolphins floated next to the *Sea Worthy* as Alena leaned over to clutch their team member tightly and lift him on board.

She hugged and patted the soaking dog before putting him down. Brutus shook himself, water fanning out from his fur in a rainbow, then immediately started barking at Chipper and Chirp. The dolphins whistled, and the three friends kept up the conversation until they realized the *Sea Worthy* was deserted.

"Tyler wouldn't dive alone would he?" Show said.

Alena shook her head. "He'd never do that. That's one of the first rules we were ever taught – " She stopped, looking at the gear locker standing open, and the missing tank and fins.

"How long do you think he's been down?" said Show.

"I don't know. But none of the tanks in here have been recharged.

If he took one of these, he doesn't have much air."

There was an explosion of water nearby.

Brutus barked furiously and jumped into the ocean. On purpose this time.

"Brutus!" Alena screamed.

Chipper stuck his long nose under the dog and flipped him onto Chirp's back. They began swimming toward something splashing around on the surface.

In a flash the girls launched one of the *Sea Worthy*'s life boats and rowed to where Brutus now had his teeth around the strap of a scuba tank, while the dolphins held Tyler's head out of the water. Tyler coughed and gagged, and finally spewed out a cup of salt water.

Crying and laughing, Alena and Show muscled him into the lifeboat, helping Brutus scramble aboard right behind him.

As Tyler tumbled over the side, he looked up at them, shaking his head, trying to clear water out of his ears. He coughed up more seawater and said, "How did I get here? I was dreaming. The last thing I remember is a flying carpet – "

A fountain of water erupted next to the boat.

The team watched in awe as a huge manta soared out of the sea, its powerful wings glistening in the sunlight. For a moment, the dark moustache shape gleamed on its pale belly. Then with a terrific splash, the magnificent creature hit the water and disappeared from site.

And Tyler knew. Knew that it hadn't been a dream. That somehow the manta had lifted him, carried him on its broad, strong back, out of the water and back to life.

EIGHTEEN

LOOSE ENDS

Café Xochitl Langosta con Mantequilla was the special aboard the *Sea Worthy* that evening. Show knew the twins loved to eat lobster and had put one on dry ice kept hidden in her backpack until now. One big enough to feed the whole team, including Brutus.

In between bites, butter dripping down his chin, Tyler was telling Show and Alena about cutting the manta loose.

"I love you for it," Alena said. "But if you ever go off by yourself and try to be the hero again, I'll – I'll – "

"And if she doesn't, " said Show, "I will."

After bringing Tyler back aboard, Show had talked to the Naval base. They had caught up with the illegal fishing boat and were escorting it into port. It wouldn't be fishing again for a very long time, if ever. The base had also sent out several boats to reel in the drift net, and it was no longer a threat.

The Foundation had gotten important data from the GPS transmitter on Moustache Pete.

"I wonder where he is now," said Tyler.

"And if Teardrop had her baby," Show said.

Alena smiled. "We'll probably never know."

Just then Brutus bounced up from the floor and barked excitedly. The twins looked at each other.

"Oh, no," they said together as the SOS alert sounded.

GLOSSARY

Algae
Any of a group of mainly water organisms that range in size from microscopic single-celled forms to multicellular forms up to 30 meters long (kelp is a type of giant algae). Once considered to be plants, they are now classified separately because they don't have true roots, stems, or leaves.

Aztecs
Refers to certain ethnic groups of central Mexico. The Aztecs dominated much of Mexico from the 14th century until the Spanish colonization of the Americas early in the 16th century. At its height, the Aztecs had a rich culture with remarkable architecture and art. Mexico City was founded on the site of the ruined Aztec capital of Tenochtitlan when Spaniard Hernán Cortés defeated the Aztecs under the leadership of Moctezuma II in 1521.

Bahia
The Spanish word for bay.

Database
A computer database is a large, structured collection of records, or data. By inputting questions, a user can retrieve answers. The A.I. Team might ask," How many giant mantas were killed in the Eastern Pacific ocean this year?" or, "Compare the picture of this boat with others and tell us who owns it and its home port."

Isla
The Spanish word for island.

Kilo
Abbreviation of kilogram – a gram is a unit of weight in the metric system. Kilo means one thousand. A kilogram is 1000 grams. One kilogram is approximately equal to 2.205 pounds.

Liter   Sometimes spelled litre, and abbreviated L, is a measure of volume used in the metric system. 1 L is equal to 1.056688 US quart and 0.2641720523 US gallons.

Plankton
Any tiny, drifting organism that lives in the ocean or fresh water. Plankton might be the most important life-form on Earth because of the food supply they provide to most of the other creatures that live in the water.

Plexiglas
A light, transparent, weather-resistant plastic.

Pod
Refers to a social group of cetaceans – whales, dolphins, etc.

Power-sled
A small underwater platform with a motor, designed to carry equipment.

Red tide
A brownish-red discoloration of marine waters caused by the presence of enormous numbers of certain microscopic plankton, that often produce a potent poison that accumulates in the tissues of shellfish, making them poisonous when eaten by humans.

Servo
A servomechanism – an electronic control system in which a hydraulic, pneumatic, or other type of controlling mechanism is activated and controlled by a low-energy signal.

Smartboard
A large, touch-controlled, interactive whiteboard made by the company SMART Technologies, which works with a projector and a computer. The whiteboard is an input device that users can write on with a digital pen, or even a finger.

Takeoff checklist
The list of things on an airplane that have to be checked for proper operation before takeoff.

United Nations
The international organization, headquartered in New York City, which aims to get countries to cooperate on law, economic development, social progress, and human rights. Currently 192 countries are members of the UN.

Volcano
An opening in the Earth's crust which allows hot, molten rock, ash, and dust to escape from deep in the planet's interior. Volcanoes are usually found at the intersection of the plates that form the Earth's surface. Many islands are formed by volcanoes which continually erupt, depositing rock, which cools and builds up over many thousands of years.